LOVING THE WHITE BILLIONAIRE 3

BY MONICA BROOKS

Copyright © 2015 by Monica Brooks

This is a work of fiction. Names, characters, places, and incidents either are the product of the author's imagination or are used fictitiously, and any resemblance to any persons, living or dead, business establishments, events, or locales is entirely coincidental.

Loving The White Billionaire 2

All rights reserved.

This book is protected under the copyright laws of the United States of America. No part of this work may be used, reproduced, or transmitted in any form or by any means, electronic or mechanical, including photocopying, recording and faxing, or by any information storage and retrieval system by anyone but the purchaser for their own personal use.

This book may not be reproduced in any form without the express written permission of Monica Brooks, except in the case of a reviewer who wishes to quote brief passages for the sake of a review written for inclusions in a magazine, newspaper, or journal—and these cases require written approval from Monica Brooks prior to publication. Any reproduction or other unauthorized use of the material or artwork herein is prohibited without the express written permission of the author.

Also by bestselling author

MONICA BROOKS

"Loving The White Billionaire"

"Loving The White Billionaire: 2"

"Loving The White Billionaire: 3"

To view these titles visit:

http://goo.gl/hCRMOY

CHAPTER ONE

"So have you talked to your family yet?" Axel asked me as we walked along the stands of the fresh produce market.

"Yes, actually, we talked yesterday while you were out with Matt."

"Did she ask you where you were?" Axel asked as he tested the firmness of a ripe tomato.

"She didn't, I guess she figured that I was still in Puerto Rico," I said as I reached for a green bell pepper.

"You're going to have to tell her eventually, you know. You can't keep me in the dark forever," Axel said before picking up and smelling a cantaloupe.

"I'm not trying to keep you in the dark, I just would rather you two meet in person," I said as we wandered further into the store for some meats.

"What kind of steak would you like?" Axel asked.

"Ribeye; that one," I said pointing to the second one down.

"Well, that's all good; except for if your family is going to give me the cold reception you got from my former friends."

It'd been almost a week since we'd been here. I'd already let my former boss know about my new career choice, and received a warm congratulations. When it came to my apartment, I still wanted to hang on to that, so I sent a money gram to my landlord. My car payments were automatically drafted as well as my insurance. Everything back at home was secure.

The only problem was with my family. Josie was okay, but Josie was my best friend, not my mother. My mother was acting as though I'd been gone for months, rather than two weeks. She'd called several times yesterday, wondering where I was and of course how I was doing. Though my mom's intentions were good, she found it hard to accept that I was an adult.

Now the pressing issue in regards to Axel was finally letting my mom know about him, firs of all, and then let her know that he was in fact white. I never had to do this before, but I guess I could start planning my speech. I needed to talk to Josie later on today. I knew that she wouldn't flip being that her father is white.

"I promise I will talk to her," I said dismissively.

"I know that you will, but when Jaida?" Axel pressed as we ordered a packet of assorted chicken.

"Axel, please don't push this issue. I will handle it; in the meantime, I just need you to trust me. Who's' to say that when I tell her about your color, that she will be any more or less accepting?" I asked as we wandered towards the pasta.

"She'll be a whole lot less shocked, that's for sure. I mean the woman doesn't even know that I exist!"

"Ok Axel, let's calm down a bit, your mom doesn't' know about me either. Are you telling me that it's more likely that you'll see my mom before I see yours?" I asked as I selected a few bundles of pasta.

"Ok, you got me there, no my mother doesn't know about you yet. Though, if you wanted to, we could chat on Skype when we get back to the house," Axel said causing me to roll my eyes.

"You always have to one up me huh?" I asked trying to control this grin.

"Oh baby, it's not trying," he said patting my bottom before walking past me.

If my legs were longer, I would've been able to kick him as he walked away laughing. Sometimes Axel could be such a smart ass.

"Axel, you're a punk," I said finally catching up to him.

He laughed and slung his arms around my shoulders, "I know," he said before pressing his lips against my temple.

"You know this all out of fear, right? It's not you, because I think you're amazing," I said as I greeted the cashier in simple Italian. I'd picked it up from Axel during the week we'd been here.

"I understand. I mean the worse they can do is kill me," he said simply.

"I realize how ridiculous I'm being, but, you're only my second lover. This is not as easy for me as it will be for you."

Axel nodded his head. Though he seemed like he wanted to say more, he understood where I was coming from. This was not going to be easy, but it couldn't possibly go as bad as I thought it could. I imagined my brothers trying to run him off, and my mom leading them into battle.

Though it seemed a little farfetched, there was some truth in my worries. The bright sun brushed our faces as we head towards the car. The weather wasn't as warm as it had been, giving us the inclination to roll down the windows. My hair flew back from my face in soft romantic curls as I ran my fingers through my silky texture.

"Who's cooking tonight?" Axel asked as we pulled up to the house.

"Well, you wanted the grilled steaks we had marinating in the fridge right?" I asked him as he turned off the ignition. His eyebrows shot upwards.

"Oh, that's right! Why did we buy these steaks then?"

"So that we can always have steaks prepared and ready for times like these," I said shrugging my shoulders.

"You're a sneaky little thing, aren't you?" he said with a playful wink.

"How about we let's get that grill cranked," I said hoping out of the car with a bounce. I smiled at him over the roof of the car.

"Ok, but you're cooking the side dishes."

"Fine by me Ax."

His eyes sparkled and his smile grew brighter before I ducked back under to fetch the groceries. As we handled the load half and half, we brushed shoulders before we walked through the doorway. Axel went straight for the back door with the charcoal he'd left by the glass just outside.

Ruffling through the bags, I started to unpack them and set them aside before preparing the zucchini. As I rinsed the vegetables, my mind began to wander. I started to think about the past week. The morning after I'd met Axel's friends, I remembered immediately how much better I'd felt compared to the night before.

My head was resting right in the nook of Axel's shoulder and his chest. My sight was obscured by his chest as it rose and fell. I watched the movement for a few moments before lifting my head. His eyes were the second thing that I saw. They were half masked, but I could tell that they were on me.

My lips lazily formed a smile as I leaned down to kiss his sturdy peck. My lungs expanded deeply as I covered my mouth. I felt the tugging of his fingers through my mossy locks and smiled when he retracted only to touch my lips.

"Good morning, beautiful," his voice caused goose bumps to make patterns down my arms.

"Good morning, handsome," I replied.

He smiled tenderly; his eyes bright as the wind brushed in through the open window. The way I felt at the moment, I didn't even remember the anger I experienced last night. It was as if he'd erased my memory during my sleep. But I did remember one thing; Axel's mention of love.

His promise of love. It made me wonder what was going on in that heart of his. Did he already love me? Or was he falling in love with me? Apparently I'd been staring too long, because he had this confused look on his face.

"What are you thinking about?" he asked inquisitively.

"Nothing..." I lied with a chuckle.

"Well, if nothing is putting that smile on your face, then I'm officially jealous," he said.

"I'm thinking of you," I started, but stopped when I thought of how he would react to his pillow talk comment.

"Oh really?" he asked suggestively.

"You're such a guy," I commented with a playful roll of my eyes.

"I have a beautiful, naked woman lying on my naked body; what else did you expect?" he asked as he pulled me into a kiss.

"This is true; I'll give you that one."

"You'll give me all of you if I asked," he stated.

I opened my mouth to refute, but I couldn't. Axel wasn't just a guy; he was much more than that. Axel was something special. My heart beat like a snare every time he came into the room. The hairs on the back of my neck rose to attention when he spoke.

"You scare me sometimes, Ax," I said.

"How so?" he asked with a bright smile.

"How you know me so well. Even after just a few weeks. You know me more than Ethan ever could; most of it is just from paying attention."

"When you're studying a subject that interests you," he said lying on his side as he repositioned us. "I mean really, interests you; it's hard not to learn every little thing about said subject," he said as his fingers caressed my lips.

"Oh yeah?"

"My favorite subject was geography. I loved to learn the beauty of the land," he said as he smoothed the skin from my abdomen to my breast. "The features and the inhabitants," he said brushing warm fingertips against my lips before gently tapping my forehead.

"I like that analogy," I said closing my eyes when he traced the outline of my cheekbone.

"Good. Now how about I make you some breakfast. I'm going to get freshened up, you do the same, and I will be back with some food."

"Sounds great."

The veggies were chopped and ready to go into the pan by the time I'd finished daydreaming. Luckily for me that I didn't slice a finger. As I cranked up the heat on the stove, I spread olive oil on the surface of the pan before I heard the sizzle of the veggies.

I focused on the sound of metal against metal and turned my head to watch Axel as he prepared the grill. Turning down the heat on the veggies, I made my way towards the door. The solid frame of the door supported my weight as I watched Axel. He'd placed the steaks down above the flames; they sizzled, crackled, and let off a tantalizing aroma.

My mouth watered, and not just because of the steak. The way his shirt laid against his sturdy chest and broad shoulders made me hungry. He looked so good manning the grill the way he did. I had to stop myself from jumping him right then and there.

His eyes flashed when they locked with mine. A smile creased his lips before he waved me over. Turning to go back to the kitchen with a plate, I crossed the yard until I stood beside him. The steaks caused my mouth to water in anticipation of a first bite. Axel was a master when it came to grilling!

Without another glance, I turned around as quickly, but carefully as I could, and made it to the table in record timing. Yelling out towards Axel to grab the veggies off of the stove, I took a seat and waited for Axel to join me.

"Wow, I've never seen you so excited; you forgot a second plate, drinks, and silverware."

"I'm sorry; all I was worried about at the time was the steaks," I said with a chuckle.

"Ok honey, we'll get you squared away."

"So," I said after slicing in and taking a juicy bite, "I guess you're still serious about the status of your relationship with Dillon and Jeremy."

"Yes, we're done," he said plainly while taking a bite of his steak.

"You know how I feel about that."

"I understand that, but I have already made my decision," he said.

"Ok," Was all I said before Axel changed the subject.

I knew that he didn't want to talk about it, but I did. These are people who he has known for many years. To drop them because of their opinion of me is huge. I know that Axel is very fond of me, but I would like to know how much

CHAPTER TWO

"I wanted to take you to Venice tomorrow," Axel said as we walked the beach hand in hand. Axel had gotten a new bikini for me as a gift. It was navy blue, and crisscrossed in the front. It flattered my curves and contrasted well against my brown skin.

"Oh? How far away is that from here?" I asked him as I side stepped a spiky seashell.

"About three hours."

"Wow, so we'll staying in Venice for a little while I'm guessing," I said with a smile.

"Just a couple of days; I think you'll like it."

"I'm pretty sure I will."

"You haven't been there before, right?" he asked.

"No. When I went with my dad that time, it was to Sicily."

"Oh, how did you like that?" his footsteps playfully toyed with the sand as we stood still.

"It was beautiful. We didn't stay in anything lavish, but, the view, the culture; everything was amazing."

"My mom would love to hear you say that. She's very proud of her culture," he said against my forehead as we stood, palm against palm. He laced his fingers with mine before he spoke.

"She has every right to be. And so do you."

"Of course. We all do," he said palming my face before taking my mouth in a slow and tender kiss.

"Mmm," I commented.

"Like sugar," his tongue slid over his lips.

"Is this a private beach?" I asked him as I began to run my hands along his body.

His smile brightened his irises as his laugh lines made their sexy appearance. My bottom lip was between my teeth as I held onto his neck. He held my waist snugly as he laid me against the warm beach sand. His hands groped my chest before he laid his hand against my neck.

"In fact, it's mine."

***

Going to Venice was like traveling to a new world. Although we were still in Italy, it was like fishing in West Virginia, and then dining in New York. The smell was different, the atmosphere had changed, and most of all, the look was transformed. We'd arrived not too long after one; we'd left a quarter till nine.

I was a little tired from travel, so Axel had rented a small riverside villa for us. It was gorgeous which is nothing less than what I expected. Though it was considerably the smallest location yet, It still quite spacious.

Axel decided to go out and get fixings for a late lunch while I stay in the hotel and slept. He wasn't gone for five minutes before I curled up in the bed. I drifted off into a nice deep slumber.

When I woke up, I heard rustling in the kitchen, and figured it was Axel preparing lunch. I decided to stay warm for a little bit longer. This bed was hugging me better than my own mother, and I didn't want to leave its embrace just yet. My stretch caused a moan to escape from my lips, my muscles quivering against the strain.

"Are you awake in here, baby?" Axel asked as he poked his head into smile at me.

"I'm just soaking up this warmth."

"Here, let me open the windows and blinds for you."

Warm sunlight spilled in like fine wine. My skin drank in its warmth and became intoxicated by the shine. I smiled and closed my eyes as I continued to relish the feeling. I wasn't used to being treated this well, but a girl could get used to feeling like a princess.

"You look so comfortable; I'm almost tempted to join you."

"Come on in, there's plenty of room," I invited.

"Don't you want to eat some lunch?" he asked as his feet led him towards me.

"I do, but what I really want is to lay here for a little while."

"Are you not hungry?" Axel said as he curled up next to me.

"I am a little. How about you bring the food in here?"

"Sounds good. I made us some sandwiches," he said before disappearing out of the room and into the kitchen. I smiled upon his arrival at sight of those sandwiches!

"Prosciutto? Oh, I love prosciutto!" I said as I held my plate under my mouth as I bit into my sandwich.

"It's prosciutto, provolone cheese, tomato salad and lettuce, on top of Italian bread."

"Axel, you spoil me likes this, and I'll never leave."

"Well, then, I know how to keep you," he said with a wink.

"That and all of the tantric sex. You keep those two up, and I'm your girl for life."

"I don't think I've ever had a girlfriend this easy going," he commented in appreciation as he slowly chewed his sandwich.

"Well, to be fair, neither have I," I said jokingly as I covered my mouth while laughing.

Axel laughed along with my corny joke and shook his head at my goofiness. I could tell that was something he loved about me with the twinkle in his eye. And there it is again: the "L" word. Love.

I found that the more time I spent with Axel, the more and more I used that word to describe things that I admired about him. I noticed how I *adored* things rather than just *liked* things.

But I didn't dare say it aloud. As a matter of fact, I found myself purposely avoiding that word around him. It wasn't like I was afraid that he wouldn't say it back. I was just afraid of hearing myself say these words.

I felt a light tap on the button of my nose and smiled when I concentrated on Axel's smile. There were times when he was the only one to be able to snap me out of my daydreaming. My active imagination was going to be the death of me one day. At least that's what my parents told me.

"I love that look on your face when you're thinking hard about something," Axel commented before collecting and deposing of our dirty plates.

"I could imagine how amusing it must look," I said.

"It's absolutely beautiful. Of course it is all the time, but especially when you are concentrating. There's something about your eyes and the way your irises seem to dance. Your eyebrows furrow so slightly, and you lips pout."

"That's beautiful to you? Because the picture you just painted in my head makes me sound like a fish!" I said with a short chuckle.

"I'm serious, Jaida. There's nothing more beautiful than a woman with a beautiful mind."

Well, I love the look you give me when I call you Ax. Your eyes light up even brighter than they are, and your laugh lines show," I said tracing one of them with my finger.

"You're making them deeper, I hope you know that," he said as he laid a peck on my palm.

"That's always a good thing to hear."

"Speaking of good things, I wanted us to go out to eat tonight, and then I have a surprise for you."

"Oh really?" I perked up when he said surprise.

"Someone looks intrigued," he commented.

"Well, you're really good at surprises, Axel. One day, I need to surprise you with something. I'm starting to feel outdone," I joked, half seriously, half not.

"You don't have to do anything special for me."

"Of course I do. Look at all of this," I said metaphorically as I monitored towards the room, "You've really spoiled me."

"Really, honey, all you have to do is keep being you, and let me have every bit of it," he said against my neck.

"Oh, you can guarantee that!"

After a lovely dinner by candlelight and beautiful sunset, Axel and I were now touring the streets. As we walked, Axel was like my personal tour guide. He knew everything about the buildings, the people, and how this place came to be.

I was so intrigued by his street savvy as we began to walk towards the canals, that I wondered how often he visited. It made me optimistic about learning this culture more extensively in the future.

I was about to ask what we were doing, when I heard the sound of a violin playing softly in the distance. At first it was like a whisper, but then it grew louder and I realized then that the person that was playing was coming closer.

I realized immediately that the person was not just a street performer, but that he was playing just for us.

Loving The White Billionaire 3

I looked up at Axel to see that he knew exactly what was going on. I smiled, hoping that he would reveal his secret when a simple red rose was held before me.

I took it gingerly in my hand as I thanked Axel. I was so confused where he got it from. By the time I went to turn around, Axel had his hand at the small of my back, and was leading me towards what seemed to be a dock.

As I got up to it, I realized that was exactly what it was, and on it stood a man dressed in stripes. Oh! A gondolier! Something that I'd only seen on TV was in living color in front of me. He extended his hand towards me, and escorted me onto the gondola.

The violinist came as well, and perched himself beside the gondolier as he began to push his way down the canal. I felt so special in the moment that I could've cried. Who else had ever done something this special and romantic for me?

I noticed with more delight that Axel had a blanket ready, some wine chilled, and fruits and cheese for a light snack. This man was too perfect, but I loved every single second of it. I curled up close to him and soaked in this moment.

I didn't want this to end. I knew that it had to, but right at that moment I felt like I was the only girl in the world. I wanted that feeling to last forever. But I didn't need all of this to make me feel that way. Every time I looked into those frosty blues, I knew that all he saw was me.

***

Though our trip to Venice only lasted a day, I was more than ready to get back to Tuscany. There was something about that house that made me feel warm. I felt more at home there than I did back in the states! Arriving back four hours later, we immediately trekked upstairs and fell into bed together.

The night before had been intense and passionate, and our long car ride did nothing but fuel the passion we had for each other. As soon as we reached the sheets, our clothes came off in an explosion of lust and heat. Our clothes lay scattered across the floor, in an array of colors, and the sheets hung off the bed by the time we were done.

"I hope you enjoyed yourself in Venice," he said as I lay on his shoulder, back against chest.

"Is that even a real concern? Of course I enjoyed myself, Ax that was the best time of my life," I said as he nuzzled his nose deep within my locks.

"That's good to hear, sugar."

"I'm so sleepy right now. You put me out every time," I commented.

"You do the same to me," he said after a huge yawn.

"I'm glad that I have that effect on you, it makes me feel special."

"Oh, you are definitely special, my dear," I heard in a whisper.

"Promise me something, Axel," I whispered back.

"Anything."

"Promise me, that no matter what happens, you won't give up on me."

He was silent for some time. I honestly thought he'd fallen asleep. Maybe he was thinking? I didn't know, but I started to feel embarrassed. The next thing I heard was a soft as a feather, I almost didn't understand it

"I will never give up on you."

CHAPTER THREE

I woke up in the middle of the night to the sound of shrill ringing. At first I didn't know what it was. That was until I ran downy he stairs and answered the telephone. I could hear sobbing and frantic voices on the other line, but I couldn't understand who they were coming from. Only two people had this number, and those two were Josie and my mother.

"Mom? Josie? Who is this?" I didn't bother to look at the caller I.D. What I did look at was the time.

"Baby! I need you to come back," the voice was cut off by muffled cries, "it's your Dad!" my mom cried.

"Dad? What's wrong with Daddy?" I asked.

My heart was in my throat, cutting off the circulation to my head. I steadied myself against a chair as I began to sway. My mom hadn't told me anything about what happened to my dad, but I knew that it had to be serious for her to call me screaming like she had.

"We're at the hospital! Please come home," she sobbed.

"Mom, I need you to calm down; tell me what happened!" I shouted in frustration.

"It's his heart! Just come here, I have to go! We're at the hospital you were born. I love you baby, bye," and with that the conversation was over.

I had never experienced my mom like this before. She was frantic and absolutely out of it, which scared me even more. I slammed the phone back down on the hook, and darted up the stairs, nearly tripping in my attempt to get to Axel. His posture was erect when I finally reached him.

"What's going on? It's three in the morning! Are you okay?" he asked reaching for me when I walked away.

"I need you to take me back to the states! My dad is in the hospital, and from the way my mom was screaming, it's bad!"

"Alright, Jaida, calm down ok? We'll be out of here by six ok?"

I whirled around, stumbling at the speed. I glared at him incredulous as he sat in confusing on the bed. My heart was pumping and I could barely catch my breath.

"What do you mean in three hours? We need to leave now!"

"Listen to me Jaida! I know that you're worried, but the pilot doesn't wake up until five. We are about an hour from the plane ok? We're going to have to wait. In the meantime, you can pack your bags and get everything you need while I do the same," Axel said calming me down.

Closing my eyes, I took a deep breath and tried to sensibly deal with the situation. Axel was right; there was nothing that I could do at the moment. I needed to calm down. Besides the fact that there was nothing that I could do until six; I was naked.

"You go take a bath or something; I'll pack our bags and get the car ready. If we leave in under an hour thirty, we'll make it there by five instead," Axel said softly while holding my shoulders.

"You're right. It's kind of chilly out there, and my birthday suit is inappropriate."

"Right," he said with a chuckle, "Go on, I'll handle everything."

"Thank you Axel."

I walked away after fist giving Axel a squeeze and made my way towards the bathroom door. I decided on a hot shower instead. I could soak in it for a few minutes to get the tension out of my back. The water was the perfect temperature; it caused the glass of the mirror and windows to fog. I could've sworn it sizzled on my skin as soon as I stepped in.

One thing it did do was relax me. Of course not completely, but it did help me take the edge off. As I lathered the bubbles up and down the length of my arm, I found myself thinking about my dad. I especially thought about the time that we spent in this very country.

I found my eyes stinging unshed tears. My dad was the reason I never quit school, I needed him in my life. I felt so terrible about leaving the states so unexpectedly; what if I were in Puerto Rico at the time? I'd skipped town and hadn't even turned on my phone. He would've been rotting in the hospital, I wouldn't have even known.

Shaking my head to try and get rid of the thought, I focused on the good. I focused on how close we were and how I could talk to him about anything. I thought about the time when I was a teen and I thought that I was pregnant. I told him before I'd told my mom. As a matter of fact, I hadn't told my mom.

He didn't make me feel like I was a tramp or that I was stupid. He said that he understood, and that mistakes happened. He let me know that he would still see me as his little girl no matter what the outcome. Turned out that I wasn't pregnant.

It was all cleared up in a matter of weeks, so there was nothing to tell by that point. But my mom did feel upset, when later she found out from Dad, that I hadn't told her. But the thing was, it wasn't about her. It has always been about my dad and I.

"Hey, I shot a text to the pilot about thirty minutes ago, and he's awake. You almost done with that shower?"

"How long have I been in here?"

"About thirty minutes now."

"Oh," I must've been thinking really hard, "I'll go get dressed," I said reaching out towards the shower nozzle.

"Ok."

"Did you need to hop in?" I asked backing away from the nozzle and hopping out.

"Here, I took this out of the dryer; I thought you might appreciate it," he said as I wrapped the warm towel around my cold body.

"It's like heaven, thank you, Ax," I said before kissing him on the cheek.

"You're welcome Jay."

The towel felt like a hug around my body. Axel was a life saver. I smiled before he kissed me on the cheek and hopped in the shower. I knew that I would be crying by the end of the day, so I decided to keep a fresh face, and just lathered a small amount of coconut oil on.

I pilled my curls on top of my head, got dressed, and headed downstairs. I figured that I would tidy up the kitchen, making sure that there wasn't anything that could attract insects on the counters. My mind must've been seriously flustered; I couldn't even remember who cleaned the kitchen last night.

The counters were spotless and the floor was mopped. There was nothing in here for me to do. Maybe the living room needed something done to it. I shook my head; there was nothing in here for me to do. I decided to check the bathrooms, all three of them. I felt the tears building as I realized that we had only used the one since we'd gotten here.

I knew what I was trying to do, and the fact that it wasn't working was getting to me. I started thinking about my dad, and how I'd left him. I thought about all the calls I could've made to him in the past, and I thought about how I might not make it to him in time. The thought broke the dam, flooded my thoughts, and trickled down my face.

I perched myself on top of the counter, and tried to collect myself. My hands were covering my face as I breathed into my palms. My body convulsed with sobs that soaked my hands and drenched my face. I needed to stop, but I couldn't.

What if last month was the last time I got to see my dad? I cursed myself for being so neglectful. Footsteps sounded, and then ended before I felt arms around me. His chest supported my weight as I melted into him. I took deep breaths, but each one broke off into a sob.

Though I cried, for maybe ten minutes now, Axel never once told me to stop. He never once told me to get a grip on myself. He just held me tight, and let me cry. He let me get out all that I needed to before I calmed down. He held me against him like he could stand there forever.

"The car is started, our bags are packed; we'll leave whenever you're ready, but no sooner," he said softly against my curls.

"I'm ready; we need to get there as soon as possible," I said after clearing my throat.

"Okay honey, let's go."

Nodding my head in compliance, I was helped down from the counter, and escorted towards the door. Axel stopped me before we reached the car door. He turned me to face him before he planted a kiss on my forehead.

"Don't let those thoughts flood your head. We're going to get you to your dad."

"Okay," I said softly.

Loving The White Billionaire 3

"I'll be next to you the whole time. Everything will be okay."

"Ok honey, let's go," I said nodding my head and showing him that I was fine.

Once we were in the car, Axel pulled out nearly as fast as he could, and shot off towards the airport where our flight awaited us. As we drove, I found my mind trying to binge on the negative thoughts again, but I quieted them with Axel's reassuring words. I decided to close my eyes, and try and get some sleep before we made it to the states.

Chapter Four

The first thing I did was hug my mother. Her arms were like a vise around me. My tears mimicked the Niagara Falls as they made patterns down my cheeks. My brothers hugged me one by one before I finally made it to my dad.

I began to sob as I reached my hand out to touch his face. He wasn't even awake. Poor thing must've been too exhausted from his heart. I bent down to wipe the tears off his face before I kissed him. I rested my head on his shoulder and I prayed, for the first time in a long time. I needed my dad, I needed him to be ok, and I needed him in my life. Finally straightening up, I turned to my mom.

"Tell me what happened?"

"He woke up coughing something terrible. I thought it was just his cold messing up again, so I went to the cabinet to fetch him some medicine," she paused for a moment and tried to collect herself.

"It's okay Momma," Sammy comforted.

"He was gagging, and blue! And I knew then that this was not just some cough."

"What's wrong with his heart?"

"Just heart failure. He's eating too much fried foods, getting old, and not exercising," she stated with a defeated shrug.

"Well, what have you been feeding him? He only eats your food!" I pointed out.

"Apparently, he's been eating over at his sister's house because *I* have been cooking too clean for him! That's what he decided to tell me before he passed back out," she said choking up towards the end.

"Oh Daddy! Why did you have to be so stubborn?"

"Can we address the elephant in the room?" Lucas asked suddenly.

It just dawned on me that I had not come alone. This was the moment that I'd feared. Damn! I should've had a better game plan than this. I was so worried about my father that I completely forgot about the introduction.

"Family, this is Axel; he brought me here from Italy."

"Italy?! What the hell were you doing in Italy?" Samuel asked.

"With a man other than your fiancé!" Lucas added.

"Oh my God! The wedding was called off!" I argued.

"And for a reason none of us know!" Lucas snapped.

"And can I ask what this man means to you? He better be the pilot!" Samuel added.

"Excuse me!" my voice echoed throughout the room.

"There's no excuse for you!" Samuel interrupted.

"Stop yelling! Maybe you all have forgotten that your father is in the hospital, but I have not! If you want to continue to yell, you can do it elsewhere."

"Ok fine, let's use our *inside voices*," Luke said sarcastically.

"And you can start, Jaida, by telling us who this man is to you."

"My name is Axel, and I am Jaida's boss," he said speaking for the first time. His voice caused the air in the room to stand still. It was so deep and authoritative; it put my mind at ease.

"I thought your boss was female?" Mom pointed out.

"She was, until I started working for Axel."

"And you met him on your honeymoon?" Samuel pointed out judgmentally.

"On my *vacation*; Ethan and I broke up remember?" I said.

"Still, I mean you break off your relationship, you leave to Puerto Rico on a whim, and then you hook up with him?" Lucas said in all seriousness. "Don't think we don't know what you meant by being my little sister's new boss, you nasty son of a-"

"You better stop that cussing! I don't tolerate that!" My mom said while she popped Samuel in the mouth like he was five.

"Momma!" Sammy complained.

"Don't talk to him that way; he's been very good to me since Ethan," I defended while walking over to stand next to him.

"He's the rebound guy, he could be pimping you out on the streets and you'd have googly eyes."

"Samuel Jackson Peterson!" Mom chided.

"Yeah, calm down," I spat.

"That's enough out of all of you! We will talk about this later, in the meantime, I would like for you *all* to get me something to eat, and you *will* get along!"

Some task my mom set us all on. My brothers didn't start any arguments, but they didn't speak either. Every now and then, I would catch them looking over at Axel, just for a moment before looking away. Axel on the other hand was totally complacent.

He didn't seem at all bothered by the immature behavior that my brothers were exhibiting. He actually seemed quite amused. At certain points, I could tell that he felt that it was actually sort of funny. In a way it was; these men were in their thirties and were acting like they are in high school.

"Are you hungry?"

"Yeah, Jaida, are you hungry?" Luke asked stepping closer in a goofy sort of manner.

"Luke, don't make me drop you in this food court," I warned with a pointed finger.

"Ooh, like I'm scared," Luke said taking a step backward.

"So, Axel. What is your last name?" Samuel asked.

"Frost," he answered politely.

"That sounds familiar. As a matter of fact...you look familiar too," Samuel said while rubbing his jaw.

"Oh snap, that's the man that we were looking at in the Forbes magazine!" Luke said in awe.

"Yes, that's him. The creator of frost computers."

"The billionaire!" Luke's facade finally broke. The only thing about Luke that bothered me was the fact that, only for moments he was truly himself. The rest of the time, he followed Samuel. I knew that Luke was upset about Ethan and I, but I knew that he wasn't as upset as he let on.

"Billionaire or not, you'll never be good enough for our little sister."

"That's right," Luke said remembering whose side he'd taken.

"Of course not. I fully understand," Axel said towards Sam who'd sucked his teeth.

"Sammy stop it!" I said.

"You just go ahead and take this back to Momma," he said handing me her plate of food before turning around, "I don't feel that I'm ready to accept this."

Just following suit, Luke lost interest and walked away. Rolling my eyes, I looked down at the container of salad for my mom. I was so annoyed that I didn't feel a sturdy hand on my shoulder. Turning around, I looked up and into shimmering eyes.

"Don't let it get to you. You saw how your brother Lucas reacted to me. He doesn't dislike me, but your brother Samuel does. Only because I am the new guy who happens to be involved with his kid sister," Axel explained the situation.

"I know, but it's annoying nonetheless."

"I actually find it kind of amusing," Axel said leaning his shoulder against me playfully.

"Of course you do. What are you up to?" I asked measuring his expression.

"Why do you ask sweetie?" His tone failed at innocence.

"Axel, please don't get in their heads. I know my brothers can be jerks but, I love them," I said.

"I won't do anything you're not comfortable with. I'll just keep quiet."

"Ugh! Axel, that's not what I meant. I just don't want you to push them too much."

"No, I understand; don't worry," he said with a wink.

Smiling as we walked back towards the hospital room, our steps were in sync, and our hands were linked. I'd laughed about a hundred times before we'd gotten back to the room. Axel made sure that even though this was hard for me, he kept me smiling.

My mom's eyes were scrutinizing as she looked down at our hands as we entered the room. I felt uncomfortable. Sliding my hand out to offer my mom food, I hoped that I didn't offend Axel. I tried to make it seem like I needed my hands. It was stupid, but I wanted to keep the peace. Taking a seat next to my mom, I kept my eyes busy on everything else but Axel.

"Where are your brothers?" My mom asked just as I was about to speak.

Loving The White Billionaire 3

"Um, I don't know; they left us in the cafeteria," I mentioned.

"Why? What did you say to them?" she asked me.

"Nothing!" I said in confusion.

"No; you're brothers love you! They would have to have a good reason to walk away from you."

"I know they love me," I said looking down at my hands.

"They are not too fond of me," Axel answered as she directed her sight towards him.

"Well, we were very fond of Ethan. It is shocking to see you here in his place."

"Yes ma'am that's understandable."

"And by that same token, I'd never heard of you until today," Mom said looking over at me.

"I knew this was going to happen," I said.

"It possibly would've been better had you given us a heads up."

"I highly doubt that giving you a heads up would've been any better."

"Your brothers still don't know why you two split in the first place!" my mom argued.

"They don't need to, remember? Besides, I don't think that would make the situation any better," my arms crossed under my chest.

"You could've at least told us that he was white."

"Mom!" I said incredulously.

40

"Your friend is part white so I understand the curiosity..."

"Mom, stop! That's really offensive."

"Don't you mom stop me, he knows he's white," Mom said as Axel nodded his head in agreement.

"Axel!"

"I am honey. I've come to terms with it," Axel said causing my mom to giggle.

"Geez Axel," I said through one of my own.

"Thought I'd lighten the mood a bit," Axel said genuinely.

"I understand more why she likes you. You are funny," My mom commented.

"Thank you."

"When is he going to wake up? Is sleeping this long normal?" I asked chaining the subject.

"The doctors just told me to let him rest," she said standing up to touch his face.

"How long has he been out?" Axel asked.

"Oh, about three hours now; not too long before you two showed up."

"And you said he passed out? Was it from exhaustion?" I asked her.

"Partially, it wasn't like he just went to sleep, he had a few words before he went out," Mom said with a chuckle.

"I bet he was blaming Sam and Luke huh?"

"You know it; they are always on his bad side."

"Just like I'm always on yours."

My mom gave me a look that told me she almost had no idea what I was talking about. But then the look faded, and was replaced with guilt. She didn't say anything, only smiled and shook her head to keep the mood light.

Though that was short lived when my brothers came back. They slid in the room without a glance or a look in Axel's direction. Rolling my eyes as I came to stand by my mom and dad, I watched my mother's fingers as they wrapped around my father's. It was such a sweet embrace, yet so simple. I smiled slightly when I thought about what that meant to them.

It was like every time their banded hands met, it was like re-sealing their vows every time. I looked away from them before my eyes met with Axel's. He didn't smile, but I could see the happiness in his eyes when he looked at me.

CHAPTER FIVE

Axel and I were on our way to my apartment in the city. The doctor had reported that my dad needed his rest and that they only allowed one overnight guest at a time. My brothers went back to Mom's house to get her some clothes, and also to stay there so that it wouldn't be empty. On the way home, we stopped at a fast food joint and were now eating in the living room.

Compared to every hotel and even Axel's home in Tuscany, my home was by far the least impressive. I noticed immediately when I turned the lights on. Though I was proud of my little apartment, still, I felt a little self-conscious. Though in Axel fashion, he put my mind at ease by how comfortably he'd slumped down on my couch, and kicked his feet up on the coffee table.

"This is the most comfortable place away from home by far!" he'd said before diving into his burger.

"I'm really glad you think so, I was a little worried."

"Don't be, you've done a great job with this place," he said approvingly.

After we finished eating, we decided to stay up and watch a scary movie. I'd never been able to watch anything like this with Ethan, and it was a very nice change. There were several points of the movie that Axel had to calm me down, and pull my hands away from my eyes. There was one point where I even jumped and screamed, to Axel's amusement, of course.

When the movie finally came to an end, I felt the need to watch something less scary, and more childlike. It was always something I did to help me sleep at night. Axel thought it was cute how I watched the cartoons like I was genuinely interested in them, but I was.

"You're adorable, you know that?" he asked.

"Oh come on, like you don't watch cartoons?"

"Not like that. I used to be hooked on watching Popeye. But I stopped after my dad died; he reminded me too much of him."

"That must've been hard for you to deal with."

"It was at first, but at the same time it wasn't," he said.

"I remember the story you told me about how he buried your dog. I got the message then."

"Yeah, he wasn't a very kind man, but he was my father," Axel's hands were in my hair as he spoke.

"So, speaking of family, do you want to run away yet?" I asked.

"Are you kidding me? You're brothers crack me up. They will come around eventually because they love you," he told me with sincerity.

"Let's get to bed; I think if I stay up any longer I'll pass out on this couch," I said before releasing myself from his grip.

"Ok, honey, lead the way."

I realized that I hadn't tidied up before I'd left for Puerto Rico. There were bras hanging up on the knob of my bathroom door, a thong dangled from the corner of my closet door, and there were magazines all over the bed.

Flying around the room like a tornado, I all but avoided eye contact with Axel until I was done. Every place that I'd been to with Axel was spotless, even his home in Tuscany. So to come here to a less than clean place was a little out of order and not to mention embarrassing.

Axel laughed and undressed as soon as I was finished. Our clothes were still in the trunk of the car, but none of us were in the mood to go get them. So instead of pajamas, we settled for just our underwear. Curling up under the sheets for comfort, we finally made it to sleep.

***

I awoke at exactly nine AM. As soon as my eyes were open, that was it. Sleep left my body, and I was ready to get going. I had to go down to the hospital to see my dad. Sitting up in my bed, I turned to look down at Axel to notice that he was still sleeping. I didn't want to wake him, so I gingerly made my way towards the bathroom to start getting ready.

By the time I was finished, Axel still had not woken up. Reaching out to grab my notepad from the bedside table, I found a pen and wrote a message to him. Leaving it on my pillow, I kissed his cheek and made my way to the door.

I had completely forgotten about the luggage in the trunk until I arrived at the hospital. There was nothing that I could do about it now. As I walked, I started thinking about my family and their reaction. I wondered how relaxed they would be and how easier it would be with just me here.

Though I instantly felt guilty for thinking that. For actually feeling relieved that Axel was not going to be there made me feel like a bad girlfriend. Though truthfully, I just wanted to enjoy my family without having them strung so high.

When I entered the room, I noticed immediately how different the family was. They were calm, there was no hostility, and I felt like I had my family back. Samuel even gave me a hug, while of course Lucas followed suit. When I got to my mom, she threw her arms around me and kissed my cheek.

My dad was still sleeping, but my mom said that he did wake up that night and stayed up with her until the early morning. I was relieved that he wasn't in some sort of coma. I took a seat next to my dad on the bed. The boys were watching, while mom hummed a melodic tune while crocheting powder blue yarn.

"So how have you been? I know you're tired," I commented on the bags under her eyes.

"Oh well you know, I got a few hours here and there, but I'm ok," she said.

"Well, if you need to go home and take a nap, Sam, Luke, and I can just stay here and wait for him to wake up."

"That's ok baby. I'm doing just fine," she said sleepily.

"So," Samuel asked while bringing over a chair, "Where's white boy?" he asked, his chocolate brown head glistening in the sunlight.

"He's back at my place," I answered.

"Oh! I thought we'd run him off," Sam said while Luke turned to join in on the conversation.

"Not even close; he didn't even know that I'd left," I said trying to defend him.

"Well, ain't that suspicious," Luke commented.

"It's not even like that."

"Then why did you leave without waking him up? Are you sure you're just not realizing how pointless this relationship is?" Samuel pointed out.

"I'm not having this conversation with you," I said, and abruptly stood to storm out of the room.

I hated when my brother thought he knew what was best for me. He was only older than me by four years, what gave him the right to comment on my life? I reached into my back pocket for my phone. The time was ten thirty, and I noticed that Axel had not yet woken up.

That or he was too angry to call me after I'd just left him. I instantly regretted my decision to leave him alone. This made me look really suspicious, although I truly hated to admit it. Maybe it wasn't suspicion, maybe it was a fact.

Maybe Samuel was right about the whole situation. I felt very strongly for Axel, and he felt the same, but we have only known each other for a short time.

My phone buzzed, snapping me out of my negative thoughts and grabbing my attention. I felt my stomach drop to my knees before I slid the button to answer the call.

"Good morning, Axel, how did you sleep?"

"I slept ok, how about you honey?" he asked. His voice was light and friendly.

"Great, I woke up early…"

"So you decided to go to the hospital instead of waking me up to go with you," he stated simply.

"I'm sorry; I just didn't want to wake you."

"You could've at least theft my clothes for me. I realize that our relationship in public and social situations is going to be hard at first; that's why we have to face those obstacles together."

"I know."

"I don't want you to take the easy way out of things like these, because that's cheating both of us," Axel said truthfully. I knew what he was saying was right.

"I'm coming home, and then we'll come back together around dinner time."

"How long have you been there?" he asked concerned.

"Just a little over an hour; my brothers are there, they'll keep my mom company."

"Did something happen?"

"Snakes on a Plane was just running his mouth again."

"Haha! You and your Samuel Jackson references!" Axel commented with a hearty laugh.

"I've done that since I knew who Sam Jackson was. I just always thought it was weird that my mom would name him after the movies star. You know how embarrassing that is?" I said trying to keep my laughter down so I could be understood.

"I nearly died trying to keep it in the first time. I could feel my face turning red," Axel laughed.

"Sorry, I'll try and keep it under wraps so you don't lose composure."

"Haha! Thank you, I appreciate that."

"Are you hungry, Ax?"

"A little bit, I've wanted some Denny's for a while now."

"Oh good, there's a Denny's right across the street from the apartments."

"Sounds like a plan."

"I guess you can get ready once I bring you your clothes," I said.

"Don't feel too guilty, I can at least take a shower."

"Ok, be there in ten."

When I got to the apartment, Axel was dressed in boxer shorts. I was surprised; had he gotten those throughout the night? Closing the front door behind me, I walked in closer to scrutinize them. They felt new. Where had he gotten new underwear from?

"You had a pack of underwear under the bed along with some shirts, some pants, and shoes. Were they for Ethan?"

"Actually no, they were for his brother. He'd stored them here one weekend so his brother wouldn't find them, but we forgot. Anyways, they're up for grabs."

"Cool deal."

"You're going to look so sexy in these," I said with excitement as I pulled out the outfit and set it on the bed.

"You think?"

"Yeah are you kidding me? This dark blue jacket, those blue eyes and these slate gray pants, are definitely going to contrast well and show off that bod," I said with a wink.

CHAPTER SIX

We both turned heads as we walked down the street to Denny's. We'd parked the car not too far from the restaurant, and decided the fresh air would do us some good. Sitting down at the booth, we ordered our food and waited for its arrival.

"I figured that we'd bring Chinese food since my mom loves it so much."

"I'm sure she'd like that."

"They haven't called me since I left though."

"Did you not let them know you were leaving?" Axel asked before taking a sip of his coffee.

"Not exactly. Sam and I got into it, and I just stood up and walked out. I probably missed my Dad waking up," I said with a frown.

"You'll get to see his eyes eventually, honey, I'm sure of it."

Axel reached out his hand to rest it against mine in comfort. His reassuring outlook put me at ease for

Loving The White Billionaire 3

the moment before our food came to the table. As we ate, we actually discussed quite a different topic, which was my job status. Axel told me the parameters of what he wanted to be done, and what needed to be done to run the company's accounts smoothly.

It didn't seem too different from working at the law firm, save for the legal jargon. I noticed immediately that this was going to be a challenge for me at first. But I accepted challenges as they came to me. I was looking forward to my first day at the company. I asked him when I would be starting, but he only gave me the date of my interview.

"So what if I don't pass the interview?" I asked honestly.

"I have faith in you that you will, but if you don't, I can still have you do accountant work at one of my other smaller businesses. You'd be making the same exact amount, though you wouldn't be able to travel as much."

"I'm hoping that you feel enough confidence in me to work for you," I said thinking about the farm house back in Tuscany.

"I have the utmost faith in you, Jaida. You're smart, your head is on your shoulders, and you have remarkable intuition. I'm pretty sure you'll pass my interview," Axel said before tossing back the rest of his coffee.

"Aren't you a box of compliments?"

"They're not compliments; so much as they are truths. But regardless, you're welcome."

"Your check, I'll take those plates for you," the waitress said before disappearing behind the counter.

We quickly made it out of the restaurant and down the street to my car. Just as I reached the door to open it, Axel snatched me into his arms, and took my lips in a deep and hungry kiss. His body was pressed firmly against mine as my back met with the cool metal of the car door.

My temperature rose against the temperature of the atmosphere. My skin tingled with every touch and every flick of the tongue. I moaned against his firm grasp, and just before we got to the point of no return, Axel broke the embrace with a smacking of lips and heavy breathing.

"Holy crap Axel, what was that?" I asked.

"A preview of tonight when I get you home," he said seductively against my lips before rubbing his hard length against my belly.

"I love when you do things like this. It's so erotic," I said my bottom lip between my teeth.

"I'm glad, because there's more where that came from," he said before giving me a firm slap on my bottom.

"Damn Ax...What was that?" I asked.

"I think your phone vibrated the second my hand connected."

Reaching into my back pocket, I pulled it out to notice that Luke was calling me. When I answered the phone, his voice was muffled. I thought that maybe it was my phone, so I walked away to try and get some signal.

"Lucas?"

"Yeah, Jaida, can you hear me?"

"Yeah, is everything ok with Dad?"

"Yeah, he just woke up. I thought I'd let you know so you can come and see him."

"I'm on my way!" I said, and hung up the phone with a quick thank you.

"Your dad woke up?" Axel asked excitedly.

"Yes, we have to hurry before he goes back to sleep!" I said getting in the driver's side before Axel got in.

Backing out of the parking space, I barely drove within the speed limit. I weaved in and out of traffic, and ran every yellow light. Nothing was going to stop me from seeing my dad. When we finally arrived at the hospital, Axel suggested that I pull up front, while he stayed behind to find a parking space.

Complying with his great suggestion, I jumped out of the car, and ran through the doors of the hospital. I tried not to run through the halls like a child, but my excitement was way too strong. When I finally got in the room, my dad was laying on the bed with his eyes on the TV.

"Daddy," I said as I came closer.

"Hey baby!" he said weakly, but excitedly.

"Oh, I'm so glad I got to see you before you fell asleep again."

"Well, you caught me just in time. This medicine they have me on is whipping my butt," he said before taking in a huge yawn.

"She came back as soon as I told her you were checked in," my mom said. I hadn't even noticed the other people in the room.

"Your Aunt was in here just a few minutes ago. She said she was upset that she missed you, and that she wants you to go by when you can."

"I will, I also want to swing by and see Josie."

"Josie…now that's a crazy child right there," Dad said as I held his hand between my two.

"She is. Are you getting tired again?" I asked as his eyes began to drift away.

"Yes, baby, I'll wake up around dinner time, just swing by and see me. I love you."

"I love you too Daddy," I said before laying his hand down by his side.

"You have a good rest, honey," Mom comforted before he closed his eyes and sleep.

"Have the doctors said anything else?" I asked after sitting down next to dad on the bed.

"He has to have surgery. There's a lot of plaque building up; they need to get it out before it becomes too severe."

"Oh no, when is it scheduled?"

"Friday at eleven."

"How is insurance covering everything?"

"Barely; his stay is going to cost us our mortgage."

"No! maybe there is something else we could do? I can help out with the hospital bill."

"Open heart surgery costs three hundred and twenty-four thousand dollars."

My eyes bugged out of my head when I heard that. I was so focused on the price that I hadn't realize that Axel was standing in the doorway. Apparently neither did anyone else. As Axel walked through the door. I heard Samuel take an exaggerated deep breath and watched Luke look away. I rolled my eyes as they curtly exchanged hellos. My mom was more polite, but still wasn't as polite as she could have been. It seemed forced.

"I went back to the apartment to get Axel once he woke up."

"I didn't know that, none of us did, you just walked out without telling any of us anything," Sam started.

"Don't start with me Samuel," I said dismissively.

"Where did you two go?" Mom asked.

"We just stopped in at Denny's for a bite to eat."

"And you didn't think to offer anything to us?" Sam asked in a manner that told me he was just trying to get under my skin.

"Don't think I didn't smell the French toast when I first got here," I pointed out.

"Why can't you all just shut up for once? Your differences in opinion should not dictate how you act in your relationships with each other," my mom interjected.

"Thank you, mom," I said sincerely.

"Now I want peace and quiet, if you have anything to say to each other, it better be something nice. If you don't have anything nice to say, shut the hell up."

With that, the room went silent, which wasn't a completely bad thing. It was actually nice for a change to hear only the sound of the TV, and occasional laughter. By the time six rolled around, my dad still hadn't woken up, but the rest of us were, and we were getting hungry.

I offered to go and pick up some food, and Samuel and Lucas decided to tag along with me. At first I thought Axel may feel uncomfortable staying with my mom, but he seemed at ease. So I left with confidence knowing that Axel would be all right.

When we got to the Chinese food store, Samuel ordered and paid for all of our meals; including Axel's and would not accept the money that Axel had offered. It was definitely a big show in pride. Though there was no contest, Samuel still had to show that he was a man.

"I don't need his money. I got my own. This is my family, not his. Just because I'm not rich does not mean I can't afford some damn Chinese food?"

"You know what, you're really ridiculous. What is your big issue?" I asked.

"The man is white Jaida! Since when have you dated white men? There's enough good black men in San Francisco?"

"It's not like I sought him out! We just happened to meet," I said crossing my arms in aggravation.

"What I don't get is the fact that you so easily went out with this guy! Especially just after calling off your wedding! It's not like you and Ethan dated for only a short time! You guys were together for so many years!" he stated.

"And things went sour and they ended! Things like this happen all the time! Why am I even having this conversation with you? I don't have to explain my love life, my life decisions, or my priorities to you!"

I hadn't realized that we were yelling until Lucas finally interjected. He placed his hand gently on my shoulder, and nudged me a little bit to snap me back into the moment. Samuel turned abruptly and collected our food before storming past me and out of the store.

Apologizing to the owners, I turned around, and made my way towards the car with Luke. When we got in, the smell of freshly made Chinese food permeated throughout the car and into our nostrils.

"I don't want you to hate me, sis. I just don't want you to get hurt," Sam said softly.

"Stop worrying about me, I'm an adult now, I'm not a little baby anymore."

"I've seen interracial relationships fail one after the other and all of them due to the fact that they deal with too much stress. Society will never accept the fact that you are a black woman dating a rich white man. You will be judged and teased and ridiculed for it. I can't protect you from that, and that bothers the hell out of me," Sam said sincerely.

"We're not telling you what to do here, Jaida, we're just hoping that you'll make the right decision," Lucas pointed out calmly.

"Thank you for your concern. I know you two love me, but you have to calm down with the protective brother instinct. Axel is a god guy. Just focus on that, please, that's all I ask," and before they could respond, I got out of the car and made my way towards the building.

CHAPTER SEVEN

On the way back home from the hospital, I found myself fixated on the words my brothers spoke from their hearts. They were trying to save me. Though they went about it the wrong way, I knew that they were just trying to protect me like they did when we were younger. When we finally got back to the apartments, Axel turned off the ignition, and sat still with me.

He was waiting for me to say or do something. Finally, I turned my head in his direction. He smiled a small smile before he reached over to touch his lips to my forehead. I smiled a ghost of a smile back, before I unbuckled my seat belt and got out of the car.

As Axel unlocked the door, I stood silently as I waited. Once we were inside, I walked straight to my bathroom, and closed the door behind me. Axel didn't bother me at first, but after thirty minutes he started to ask questions.

"What happened, Jaida?"

"Nothing, I'll be out in just a minute."

"Ok."

After ten minutes, I finally got down from the counter and faced Axel in the room. He was sitting up in the bed, his eyes locked with mine before I broke eye contact. Though I did sit down close to him on the bed. Our fingers wove together as we shared the plush space.

"My brothers are just really getting on my nerves; that's all."

"Look, how about we go to your best friend's house, Josie was it?"

"Tomorrow?"

"Yeah, how about it?"

"That does sound like a good idea; I haven't even called her since I've been here."

"There you go, just give her a call, and we'll head over there tomorrow."

"She always did help me out when it came handling my overbearing brothers," I said.

"Well good then, we'll make a trip and get your mind off of them for a while. You should call your mom to ask her to keep you informed on your dad; keep you posted on when he's awake."

"Sounds like a good idea," I said after taking a deep breath.

"Let's get some sleep, and then in the morning you can decide what you want to do."

I nodded my head in agreement, but I didn't say anything. Instead I got up, and got myself ready for bed. When I finally lay down, it was while Axel was still in the shower. I decided that I wouldn't wait up for him; I was too tired and too emotional. It didn't take me long. Axel was still in the shower when I fell asleep.

When I woke up, it was almost as if I'd just fallen asleep. I didn't feel energized at all. I felt more like I'd never gone to sleep. I felt sluggish and weak from exhaustion. It was probably a mix of stress, and all of the unhealthy food I had been eating over the past few weeks.

"Hey, I made some fruit smoothies. I figured that we've been eating a little too much fat, so I went out and bought turkey bacon and fruit."

"Wow, did you wake up feeling exhausted too?" I asked.

"A little bit. I need to go running or something."

"We could go later on tonight if you want. I like to run on the beach after the sun sets."

"Ok sounds great, I also got some other health foods, I found a ship that I'm pretty sure you're familiar with that sells health foods."

Loving The White Billionaire 3

"Yes, I go there often," I said stretching before standing up.

Heading to the bathroom, I decided to hop in the shower real quick and freshen up before breakfast. I could hear Axel saying something, but felt as though he wasn't talking to me. He carried on with his conversation, although I never responded.

"I didn't know you were in the shower. I've been talking to myself the whole time."

"Oh, sorry. I just came straight in here," I said wrapping a towel around myself before stepping out of the shower.

"How did you sleep last night?"

"I slept fine."

"Do you want to tell me why you keep giving me short answers without giving me direct eye contact?" he asked.

"What?" I felt so embarrassed that I didn't know what to say.

"I know that your brothers gave you a hard time last night, but why are you taking it out on me?" Axel asked.

"I'm not. I'm just...not," I said turning away to face the sink.

"Talk to me, Jaida."

"My brothers are only trying to protect me, Axel."

"What are you talking about? Protect you from what? *Me?*"

"From society and how they will treat us. They don't dislike you; they just dislike the stress that it will bring on me."

"I can understand that, but just because something is going to be hard, does not mean that you should just avoid it."

"I'm just so confused about what I should do, Axel. I mean, when the doors are closed and it's just us, we're in a perfect little world. But then we go out and we get stares and people looking down their noses at us! My family is giving us crap even when I'm alone and you're not there! What's the point in having the perfect relationship if we can't even celebrate it with our families?"

"Jaida, I know this is new for you, this is new for me too, but you know what, I"m not giving up on this. I am not giving up on you."

"Axel," I sobbed.

"You listen to me, Jaida, if you feel anywhere near as much for me as I feel for you, then you'll stay with me, and we'll get through this together."

"Do you really think this is worth it? Being uncomfortable around family members and out in public?"

"Yes, Jaida, you are worth it to me," he said sincerely.

I didn't say anything; all I did was look into his eyes. The truth was written in them, all I had to do was accept it. A tear rolled over my eyelid, but didn't get far as Axel caressed my cheek. My eyes closed lightly before I rested my head against sturdy muscles.

"Let's get something to eat, Jaida. And then we can get our day started," he said against my forehead.

"Ok, what kind of fruit did you get?"

"Melons, bananas, strawberries, and kiwi fruit."

That sounded delicious to my healthy side, and cheered me up to the point where the tears ceased to roll. I lifted my head from Axel's chest, and smiled when he kissed my cheeks. At that moment, the familiar rumble of my stomach caught our attention before we headed out and into the kitchen.

As I sat down at the small dining table, I watched Axel as he got to work preparing food for his baby, as he called it. As I leaned back against the hardness of the chair, I reached across the table for a soft fruit. The brown fuzz of the kiwi felt like I was holding a tuft of fur.

I brought it to my nose, tickling the tip with the texture. Taking a deep breath, the strong aroma of citrus cleared my sinuses and rejuvenated my senses.

I heard Axel say something, but I missed it. Turning to focus on him, I opened my mouth to speak when he placed a big mug of fruit smoothie down on the table next to me.

"Did you get these at the food store?" I asked while I admired the flowery design in the glass.

"Yeah, do you like them?"

"I do, I've never seen mugs this huge!" I said before taking a sip.

"How do you like your smoothie?" he asked as I closed my eyes from the full flavor.

"Oh yeah!" was all I answered before dipping my head to take another full swig.

"Good, I used raw honey as a sweetener, and there's also avocado mixed in."

"Oh, good choice," I said licking the foam off my lips.

"How about some bacon and cheese?" he said before setting the plate down in front of me.

"Wow, Axel, you really know how to make healthy foods huh?"

"That's my specialty," he answered before sitting down to join me.

"We should definitely keep this up; I'm already starting to feel much better."

"That' good. After we visit your father, we can go running on the beach if you want," he offered.

"Oh yeah, I'd like that."

"Good, I thought I could make us some lunch and then follow it up with dinner out."

"Sounds good, where?"

"Sushi?" he asked.

"Ooh! Yes, sushi! We can go to this restaurant that I've been dying to go to since it opened about three months ago!" I said.

Well then, sushi it is."

"I'm so glad that I met you, Axel, regardless of all the negativity," I said softly.

"I am too, Jaida, I am too," he said with a gentle voice of his own.

"I mean, you like the same stuff I do, you're so attentive it's almost unreal. Truly, I'm waiting for you to prove that you're not perfect. Have you killed anybody in your past?" I asked taking another sip.

"Of course not!" he said mockingly suspicious.

"Sure, because that wasn't suspicious at all."

"I'm too nice of a person to commit murder," he said.

"You know, you're right. So far you haven't had any explosions of anger so; I believe that you're too nice to kill. We'll see how long that lasts," I said with a wink.

"You're something else, you know that?"

"I do."

"Alright, hurry up, let's get you to your friends before I rip your clothes off." he said.

"Ok, Ax."

Jumping up from the table feeling brand new, I made it back to the room to throw on some shoes and a jacket, before I reached my phone. Punching in the appropriate numbers, I waited three rings before the other line picked up.

"Hello?" my mom answered.

"Hey mom, how are you doing this morning?" I asked.

"Just fine, I went home last night upon request from your father. I got some good sleep for the first time in a few days."

"That's really good to hear, Mom. We don't need both of you to be sick and in the hospital."

"That's exactly what you're father said!" My mom said through a chuckle.

"Are Sammy and Luke there?" I asked.

"No, they're on their way though."

"Oh ok, well I was going to stop by there later in the evening. I wanted to go by and see Josie, and maybe Aunt Florence."

"Oh! That sounds like a great idea. Maybe Josie can come up, I would love to see her, and I'm sure your father would too," she said.

"Yeah, I'm going to call her now and see if she has anything planned today, being that it is Thursday."

"I thought she was off Thursdays?"

"You're right! Ok mom, I'm going to call you back later on in the day, please let me know if Daddy wakes up. I love you."

"Love you too, baby, bye bye."

Pushing a few buttons on the screen, I ended the call with my mom before calling Josie. She didn't answer on the first try, but called me back before I could redial. She had me on hold for the first few moments of the call, but finally answered with a chipper greeting.

"Josie! I missed you girl!" I said in response.

"Are you back in San Fran?" she asked.

"Yes ma'am!" I said as she squealed in delight.

"Come over right now!"

"I am. Oh and by the way, I won't be coming alone…"

"You better not be back with Ethan!" She said sternly.

"I'm not! His name is Axel."

"Axel Frost?" Josie joked.

"Um, actually, yes, Axel Frost!"

"Oh, right, his name is Axel Frost, like the billionaire."

"No, his name is Axel Frost. He is the billionaire," I said.

"Ok, yeah, whatever. I'll see you and "Axel Frost" in ten minutes."

Josie hung up the phone as she tried to control her laughter; little did she know that I would have the last laugh. As I stuck my phone in my jacket pocket, Axel came up to stand next to me. He looked down at my amused expression as he tried to figure out what was so funny.

"She doesn't believe that I'm dating Axel Frost."

"Oh! Yeah, that has happened to one of my significant others before. Her parent's nearly passed out when they saw me," he said with a laugh.

"I can't imagine the look on her face."

"Oh, trust me, it'll be priceless."

Chapter Eight

Axel was exactly right. Josie's expression when she laid eyes on Axel was priceless. For a moment she was completely speechless. I had to snap my fingers in front of her face to snap her back to reality. She apologized and blushed before she stepped back into her crazy and flamboyant personality.

"Nice to meet you in person Mr. Sexy, they call me Josie," she said extending her hand.

"Nice to meet you, Mrs. Josie," Axel said before kissing the back of her hand.

Oh my God! He kissed my hand," Josie exclaimed as we all laughed at her reaction.

"Ok, that's enough from the both of you, are we allowed to come inside now?" I asked.

"Alright, come one in. I'm sure it's not the most lavish living area you've ever been in, but it'll have to do for now," Josie said.

"I don't know what it is with the both of you, but I love both of your places! You two have excellent taste in home decor."

"Oh, girl he even talks money!"

"I can see why she's your best friend," Axel complimented.

"Are you guy's hungry? I'm about to make some Mediterranean burgers," Josie said from the kitchen.

"That sound delicious, how do you make that?"

"With turkey, I've been trying to keep my eating clean. Your dad scared me."

"Oh, so you've heard?"

"Heard what?" she asked.

"Dad's in the hospital," I said sitting down in her kitchen.

"Oh my God! It's his heart isn't it?" Josie asked with her hand on her chest.

"How did you know?"

"Because he's been complaining about it. Last time I saw him, he was at the store and I heard him fussing about his cough with your mom. But what made me think it was his heart was the fact that he was out of breath and holding his chest. He tried to put on a facade when he saw me; I don't think he realized that I heard him."

"I guess I'm the only one who didn't know. Here I am living it up in the Bahamas and my dad is over here dying."

"Honey, don't do that to yourself. I'm pretty sure that he didn't tell anybody," Axel said rubbing my back.

"Exactly; you have done nothing wrong."

"I can't help but to feel that way. We barely talk because he's awake for such a short time. Apparently he's supposed to go in for surgery tomorrow."

"Open heart surgery...damn. That is one of the most expensive surgeries."

"Almost four hundred thousand dollars," I answered.

"Just make sure you keep me posted. I'll be praying for him."

"Wow, it's already two thirty."

We'd already finished our lunches by then and were now sitting in the living room enjoying each other's company. I noticed immediately that Axel was the type of person who could get along with anyone. The way he joked around with Josie with such ease, let me know that he could put up with anything.

Josie wasn't hard to get along with, but it took a special type of person to not take offense to some of her jokes. Axel laughed them off like a pro, and even had some of his own. I got up after a while to go to

Loving The White Billionaire 3

the bathroom, and as I was washing my hands my phone vibrated in my pocket.

Drying my hands off with haste, I shoved my hand in my back pocket and pulled it out to see that it was my mom. I got so excited I ran out of the bathroom and into the living room. As soon as I answered it, my excitement ran away and was replaced with fear.

"Come to the hospital, he's being rushed into surgery early!"

"What? What happened?"

"Just come down! Please!" she cried before hanging up the phone.

"Go ahead, don't worry about helping me clean up, you just let me know what's going on!" Josie said rushing us out of the house.

Jumping into the driver's side, Axel slammed the passenger door behind him, and we shot off down the road.

We'd gotten to the hospital as fast as we could. But by the time we got there, it was too late. My dad had already been whisked away for surgery. Tears instantly fell down my cheeks when I realized that I was too late.

As we stood in the waiting area outside of the surgery room, Samuel paced back and forth while Luke sat with his chin on his entwined fingers. Mom sat with her hands together in prayer as she whispered silently to the Lord.

Axel rested his hand on my back to soothe and comfort me as he rubbed it back and forth. We stood by the chairs; I couldn't bear to sit down at the moment. I was about five seconds away from pacing like Samuel.

"Hey, don't worry too much, he's in good hands," Axel soothed against my ear before hugging me.

"You know what, before I was just trying to follow my sister's wishes, but now, I don't care anything about that," Samuel started after standing still.

"What are you talking about?" I asked lifting my head from Axel's chest.

"The guilt that you feel right now could've been avoided if you weren't too far up his ass is what the hell I"m talking about!" Samuel busted.

"You can dislike me all you want to, but I'm sick of the way you keep talking to your sister!" Axel snapped.

"Oh, so now you decided to defend her? It's been almost about a week and you haven't had anything to say before."

"Because like you, I was respecting Jaida's wishes to keep my composure, but for you to say something like that shows me you don't have any respect for her request."

"You don't know anything about me, or her, being that you've only been dating for a few weeks! Who are you to challenge my respect?"

"Look, I may not have mown her for longer, but it's very apparent who has more respect."

"It's not called respect it's called puppy love. The only reason you'd do anything she says is because you're getting laid."

"Samuel!" My mom interjected.

"No, he's right, Ma. You can't tell me this man loves our sister. He's a billionaire playboy who could get anyone he wants!" Luke added.

"Lucas, I'm going to need you to stop complementing the man who is screwing baby sister," Samuel said.

"What I'm saying is, it's just a matter of time before he loses interest and tosses you to the side for another woman."

"How dare you talk about your sister that way? How dare you try and make me seem like I have those intentions for her? Do you want to know why I'm here? It's because I love her, and I would do anything and everything to makes sure that she's happy. And if that means leaving another country to make sure she sees her mother, her father, and her asshole brothers that's exactly what I'm going to do!"

That was the first time I'd heard Axel say that he loved me. The room went quiet for a moment after he said those words. I didn't know how to react to that. I felt stuck like I should say something, but the situation trapped me and prevented me from saying anything at all.

"You don't love her," Samuel said getting close to Axel's face, "You love what she does to you at night. I refuse to let you use my baby sister like she's some toy."

"The only one who's playing her right now, is you. You may not like me because I'm white, you may not like me because I'm not Ethan, but you damn sure better get used to the fact that I love your sister, and I'm not going anywhere."

Samuel scoffed and took a step back to look at me. I hadn't said anything through this whole charade. I knew exactly what Samuel was about to do by the look in his eye.

"And why haven't you said anything? This man is here defending you, and all you can do is watch? You may love her," he said while still looking at me, "But right now, she doesn't love you as much as you think."

"Samuel, stop it" I said.

"Tell me I'm wrong and I will."

Though everything within me screamed at Samuel that I loved Axel as well and that he was the one for me, my mouth never opened. The words were right there, but one thing stopped me; fear. I looked down at my shoes in shame. I could feel Axel's eyes on me, and I knew my silence hurt him.

I heard Axel chuckle humorlessly, and just as I looked up, I saw his back as he walked away. My heart immediately began to ache with pain. I just let someone amazing like Axel walk away. And I did nothing to stop him.

I couldn't bear to watch him any longer, and turned away and back to my family. Tears moistened my eyes and spilled as I tried to blink them back. My hand covered my mouth as I sobbed into it.

I heard footsteps before I felt hands against my shoulders. But they weren't the hands I'd grown to love. Anger boiled my blood hot as he tried to comfort me with a hug. Losing composure, I shoved him away from me as he stumbled towards the ground. He caught himself before he fell, and looked at me as if I'd suddenly grown a third eye.

My mom exclaimed, but I didn't pay her any attention. There was a way to protect someone without running their life in the process. I no longer saw my brother as my protector, but rather my enemy.

Maybe he was right, maybe he was wrong. All I knew was that right now, Samuel was not my brother at that moment. Lucas came to help, but stopped when Samuel righted himself. Though I wasn't as mad at Lucas as I was at Samuel, I still didn't want him near me.

The only reason I didn't leave was because my Dad wasn't out of surgery yet. I didn't want to leave without hearing what the surgeons had to say, so I sat all the way to the back of the room, and waited until the surgery was over. I didn't care how childish it seemed, I didn't want to be around the people who'd rejected Axel without so much as giving him a chance. But I couldn't just be made at them either. I had myself to blame as well for not sticking up for him.

I needed my dad. I need to hear his voice. I needed to see how he felt about it all. I'd never had this experience, but my dad was different from the rest of my family. My dad was an understanding father, and he was always in my corner.

Chapter Nine

"Mrs. Peterson?" I heard from the other side of the waiting room.

"Yes, is my husband ok?" my mom said as I came up to stand beside her.

"Your husband is doing remarkably. He's recovering right now, but he should be awake within a few hours."

"A few hours? Is that normal?" I asked.

"Generally, a patient of open heart surgery doesn't have a specific recovery rate, so we can judge how or when he will wake up. But, in Mr. Peterson's case, he should wake up sooner than later. The plaque buildup was not as severe as most men his age. Besides the need for open heart surgery, your father and husband is very healthy. He will be transferred to the CICU, but we will let you know when you can go in and see him."

Loving The White Billionaire 3

"Thank you so much, doctor," Samuel said while taking his hand in a firm shake.

"No problem, you have a great night, we'll be out again shortly to let you have some time with your father," and with that, the doctor nodded and walked away.

"Please call me when he wakes up," was all I said before I walked away from them.

I heard my mom call after me, but I ignored her as I made my way out of the hospital. I rounded the corner of the main lobby, and eventually walked through the automatic doors. I dug my keys out of my back pocket and unlocked my doors before I hopped in and drove off.

When I arrived home, I noticed that, of course, it was empty. His stuff was still there, but I knew that he could do without them. All he needed was his phone and his wallet. He probably hailed a taxi and checked into a hotel by now. I felt a pang of anxiety when I realized that he would probably be gone in the morning.

It was only three in the afternoon when Mom called to alert me that they would be performing surgery early. We hadn't been in the hospital for an hour before Axel had stormed out. I was hoping that Mom would call me before visiting hours were over.

I felt like I should reach out to him, but I was afraid and ashamed. What if he didn't want to talk to me at all? I pulled my phone out of my pocket to see if I'd gotten any calls while I was driving home. I'd turned my phone off upon entering the hospital.

When it came back on, I saw that Axel had actually tried to call me. He sent me a text message telling me to call him as soon as I turned my phone back on. I immediately called him back, and waited anxiously for him to answer.

"Jaida," he said when he picked up.

"You wanted me to call you?" I asked gingerly.

"I just wanted to let you know that I will be leaving in the morning. I know that you love me, Jaida, I do; but you're not ready for this."

"Axel-"

"Jaida, I love you," he said before hanging up the phone.

"Axel!" I yelled before tossing the phone down on the bed. I sobbed immediately, realizing that I had just tossed away the best relationship of my life. And because of what? My overprotective brothers? It wasn't as if Axel was bad for me. It wasn't as if he was the reason I didn't want to be with him.

I let someone else make the decision for me, and I had to live with that for the rest of my life. I didn't know where he was, all I knew was where the airport was. But what if I was too late to get to him?

I could only hope that he would leave later in the morning, instead of early just in case my dad didn't wake up until tomorrow. I could kick myself if it were possible. God I was so tired, but there was no way that I could fall asleep.

I decided to force myself to relax. I went to my fridge and pulled out a bottle of red wine. After pouring my first glass, I felt instantly better. After my second glass, I started to wonder why I was so upset in the first place. I wasn't ashamed to say that I was a light drinker.

Stumbling to my bed, as soon as y head hit the pillow, I burst into tears. I was sobbing as if I were a child who had just gotten a spanking. Clutching my pillow to my chest, I realized that I had been holding on to these tears longer than I should have.

The alcohol brought my emotions out of hiding with little to no coaxing. Eventually, I cried until I had no tears left to give. I got up, turned off the lights in my apartment, and stumbled back to bed. As soon as I covered up, I went to sleep.

Chapter Ten

It was six in the morning when I heard my phone screaming in my ear. I had a massive headache and felt as though I was still drunk. But as soon as I heard my mother's voice telling me my dad had woken up, the intoxication faded away. I shot straight up, jumped out of bed, got dressed, and ran out of the door.

My hair looked like straw , my clothes were dirty, and I didn't have any socks on, but I didn't care either. I needed to get to my dad. As soon as I jumped in the car, I sped off, caring little about traffic laws. Good thing there weren't any cops out to stop me; I'd made it to the hospital in record timing.

I ran through the hospital doors, past the main lobby, and slowed down as I reached the CICU. I didn't want to possibly crash into a patient. My mom told me what room to go to, but I was confused when

Loving The White Billionaire 3

I got in. Only Dad was there. My brothers were MIA as well as my mom.

But I instantly forgot when I saw my dad's eyes on me. He smiled so brightly, I wondered what he was doing in CICU. It was so strong, so powerful like he hadn't just woken up from open heart surgery.

"Daddy," I said with tears in my eyes as I leaned down to hug him.

"It is so good to see you," he said as I straightened up to look at him.

"It's good to see you too, Dad."

"Why do you look so tired? I'm the one who just had surgery, remember?" he joked.

"Oh, I just woke up. It's nothing. How are you feeling?"

"As strong as I have ever been, but I'm also a little upset with how my sons and my wife have been treating you," he said.

"What did they tell you?"

"Nothing besides the fact that you have been seeing someone else."

"His name is Axel Frost, but, we're not together anymore."

"And why is that?" he asked bemused.

"Because of an argument."

"Samuel told me he said some things…and are you telling me that's why you gave up on love?"

I felt too embarrassed to look in his eyes. I looked down at my hands and nodded my head. I didn't want it to be true, but there was nothing that I could refute. I had let him walk away because of my brother's opinion, not my own.

"Look at me," he said sternly before I looked into his eyes, "Go get him."

"What?" I asked shocked.

"If you love him, then you don't need to let anyone else get in the way of that. Follow whatever your heart is telling you no matter what, and you'll have a love that can move mountains."

"I love you, Daddy," I said reaching down to hug him gently.

"I love you too. Now go and get him before it's too late," he called after me as I ran out of the room.

My dad was right, Axel was right, and I was wrong. And I needed to get to Axel before I lost him forever. I remembered him telling me that he was leaving in the morning, and I also remember which airport we'd landed at.

The only problem was the rush hour traffic. I jumped in my car, thinking that I could turn on the radio to see how heavy traffic was this morning. I turned the key, once, then twice. But nothing happened. Slamming my fist on the steering wheel when

I realized that I'd left the headlights on, I cursed myself, jumped out of the car, and ran towards the street.

I was about to signal for a taxi when one pulled up in front of me. The back door swung open, and my heart dropped immediately. Dark brown eyes stared straight into mine.

"Hello Jaida," Ethan said.

I'd always wondered what would happen when I saw him again. Would I cry or would I scream? Would I fall back in love with him? Or would I be holding Axel's hand?

"Hi Ethan! Bye Ethan!" was all I said before jumping in the taxi and telling him where I needed to go.

I looked back and snickered at Ethan's dumbfounded expression, but turned my sights back to the road as the taxi drive merged in with traffic. Looking down at my phone, I searched for Axel's number in my phone book.

It rang and rang and rang, but Axel never opened it. I wondered if that was because he was in the air already, and I just missed my chance. I cursed under my breath. There was no way that could happen. I needed to get to him before he left!

"Sir, could you please speed up!" I said impatiently.

"Look lady, I don't know what your deal is, but there's no way I'm getting to that airport in under an hour."

"Are you sure? There are a lot of openings here on this bridge; can't you just squeeze in a little?"

"And scratch this paint? It might not seem much to you, but this is my living!"

"I know but I need to get to the airport fast, ok? IT's a life and death situation!"

"It sounds like a personal problem to me. If it was such a life and death situation then why didn't you just stay in the hospital? You're just going to have to wait!

"Shit! Listen, I need you to make an exception ok? I'll pay you extra if you can get me there in less than thirty-five minutes."

"How much extra?"

When I got to the airport, I immediately felt overwhelmed. I'd never seen the airport this packed before. I realized that it was Friday, but still, this was worse than traffic. Squeezing past a few people as I searched for Axel, I remembered exactly where Axel would go. The only problem was getting to him before he got there.

I reached back in my phone, and was shocked when I saw his name flash across my screen. I answered immediately. At first I couldn't hear him, but finally finding a break in the ongoing chaos of the airport, I asked him what he said.

"I said, what are you doing?"

"I'm looking for…wait, what do you mean what am I doing?" I asked looking around.

I was going in circles until I froze. The look on his face stopped me dead in my tracks and caused my heart to thrum deep in my chest. He looked so, intimidating. I knew that he was mad at me, but he seemed almost livid right now, instead of happy to see me.

"I'm glad I caught up to you."

"Why?" he asked.

"I…wanted to find you."

"I understand that, but why?"

Axel, I'm here, to find you because, I wanted to say that I was wrong to let you leave. And I was wrong to let my family put a wedge between the two of us. I should've said something to them. I know you're mad at me, and with good reason, but if you can forgive me, I would like for us to start again," I said as he stood three steps from me.

"Give me a reason why I should? I mean, you honestly can't expect me to give you another chance. How do I know you won't do this again?"

"I will do anything to prove to you how truly sorry I am. Axel, the day I met you, was the day you changed my life forever, and I can't imagine my life without you. Axel, I love you."

Axel tried to hide his happiness, but I could tell that those words meant a great deal to him. He looked away from me and to his left for a while, and didn't say anything. I almost felt as if I should say something, but before I could, I was swooped up and into his arms.

He kissed me fiercely and passionately as his arms held me tight against him. I felt so happy that my eyes watered with emotion. I'd never felt a love like this. Axel was mine now, and I would never let him go again.

By the time we'd gotten back to the states, it was around noon. My mom knew that we were on our way and made the necessary arrangements for our arrival. A few months had passed, and dad had made a full recovery. MY mom told me that he'd been eating a lot healthier.

He even told me that he'd been to the gym several times that week and had started a new healthy regimen. My mom said she hadn't seen him that healthy in years. I couldn't wait to see him. I missed my family, but not near as much as I missed my dad.

I knocked on the door as soon as we'd gotten out, and was greeted with a huge hug from my mom. Walking past her, I gave my Josie and her husband a hug, before finally reaching my Dad. I could hear Axel getting along with the family with ease, and smiled when my dad kissed my forehead like I was five years old again.

When I turned around to look back at Axel, I noticed that he was holding Samuel's hand in his. They were locked in that embrace for some time before Sammy gave him a hug. Lucas followed suit and embraced Axel as well.

"I hope we can have a good relationship, Sam and Luke."

"As long as you treat our sister right, we're alright," Samuel said embracing Axel once again.

"You never have to worry about that."

"After what you did for our father, paying the bill that we could never have afforded in our lifetimes, you became number one in my book," Luke said

"Oh please, you had a crush on Axel from the start!" Samuel said causing the whole family, who had been listening in on their conversation, to burst out into a fit of laughter.

"Man! Shut up Shaft!" Luke teased causing the family to continue in on the laughter.

After the family finally settled down, we all gathered around the table for dinner. Mom had prepared a healthy selection of grilled chicken breasts, and salmon along with veggies. Everything was delicious, and we were all having such a great time.

When the laughter died down for a moment, Axel and I decided that was the perfect moment to announce our surprise. Axel gathered their attention, and gave the floor to me as I held up my small hand.

"You're engaged! Oh my baby!" My dad exclaimed.

"This calls for some bubbly!" Josie called out.

"Oh Lord, somebody better get this woman away from the wine!" Sam teased.

"I'm so happy for you, you two are a wonderful couple," my mom complimented.

After dinner was over, and we'd said our goodbyes, Axel and I headed to our hotel to check-in. Since our permanent residence was now in Tuscany, I gave up my apartment and left my car with to my mother. My job interview with Axel went well, like he'd predicted, and I was signed on as a permanent employee of the company.

When we arrived at the hotel or should I say, luxury suite, I knew that something was up as soon as I opened the door. Dim light lit the room romantically. The smell of fresh roses wafted up from under my footsteps as each petal caressed my bare feet.

As I walked further into the suite, I bit my lip, and turned around to notice a huge stuffed teddy bear stood eye level with me. I'd never seen something so large in person, and I immediately reached out and took it in a warm embrace.

I looked over its fluffy brown shoulder at Axel, who held a slender black box in his hand. He opened it to reveal a white gold chain with a chocolate diamond pendant dangling at the end of it. It was so gorgeous I didn't even want to touch it.

"Don't put it on me just yet. I want to wear it tomorrow with my new dress."

Axel nodded in compliance as he placed the necklace back in its box, and set it to the side. Grabbing my teddy bear from me, he tossed it to floor, and snatched me off of my feet almost as if I were a teddy bear.

He walked easily over to the bed, and lay me down gently. His hands met with the flesh of my belly underneath my shirt, and around them rim of my low rise jeans. He pulled them down slowly kissing the flesh of my thighs as he revealed them. I sucked in my breath each time I felt his stubble scrape gently against my inner thighs.

When he was done, he came up to place his lips against my belly button. He kissed it gently twice before climbing on top of me. My shirt was up and over my head before I felt his hands as the softly caressed my breasts. I moaned as he gently revealed one nipple from the silk of my powder pink bra.

He teased it with skilled fingers as he watched me writhe beneath him. Reaching behind me, he took my bra off in a matter of seconds, and tossed it to the floor. His hands came up to grab my sound mounds of flesh before leaning down to give them both a sweet gentle peck. When he sat back up straight, he stopped his sheer torture, and for a moment, all he did was stare at me.

"You are the most beautiful woman I have ever laid eyes on. I'm the luckiest man on the planet to be able to call you my girlfriend, my fiancée, my future wife, and mother of my children."

I took in a deep breath as the goose bumps struck me as hard as those sweet soft spoken words had. I brought my hand up to cover my mouth as I looked into his beautiful eyes. The love that he was showing me was raw, it was real, and it was all for me.

It was the deepest look of love that I have ever seen in a man's eyes. I began to tear up instantly from the happiness that he bestowed upon me with those words. Axel wiped them away with his lips as he kissed me on the cheeks. He trailed them down my neck as I wrapped my arms around his. They tenderly kissed each collarbone, each breast, and my lips as he left patterns of affection down my body.

Loving The White Billionaire 3

I closed my eyes when I felt his mouth against my sex. I almost held my breath when he began to fill me with his fingers. My panties were pulled down and tossed to the side before he optioned to work on me. I felt his lips kiss me tenderly as my hips rocked against his face.

My fingers began to dig into the sheets as I called out in sweet agony. I felt my hips began to buck with my building orgasm. Axel continued to thrust his fingers in and against my g-spot, causing my walls to tremble as strong waves of pleasure erupted into a powerful orgasm.

His name rang through the room like a ballad as I sang his praises. He immediately came up to cover my mouth with a warm seductive kiss. I tasted myself on his lips before I bit my tongue. The pressure from his size entered me almost immediately after he was finished, and before he stood up. My leg wrapped around his waist before I felt the cold hard wall suddenly against my back.

My legs still wrapped around him, I nearly screamed in pleasure when he thrust deep inside of me in one hard stroke. I bit my lip and scored his back when I felt him again. My legs began to tremble as he picked up tempo, and my face began to spot with sweat as my breathing turned into full on panting.

The sound of our hips smacking together was pure and erotic as it echoed off the walls. I cried out his name more times than I can count, and moaned over and over again with each pump of his erect member. He held me to the wall like I was a nail and he was the hammer, I couldn't remember a time when I was ever so happily compared to construction tools.

I could tell that he was close. The look in his eyes was almost feral as he pressed his forehead against mine. His hand wrapped gently, but firmly around my neck as he picked up his tempo for the last few thrusts. His voice came out like a roar against my lips, I felt as though my eardrums might burst, but didn't care.

Axel's knees buckled, but he caught me before we both tumbled to the ground. I laughed as I lay sweaty and exhausted on top of him. He pat my bottom a couple of times before he gave it a nice firm squeeze. I lifted my head, and looked into his eyes to see the same look of amusement mirrored in them.

"God I love you," he said breathily.

"I love you too."

~The End~

Thank you for reading!

Also by bestselling author

MONICA BROOKS

"Loving The White Billionaire"

"Loving The White Billionaire: 2"

"Loving The White Billionaire: 3"

To view these titles visit:

http://goo.gl/hCRMOY

Made in the USA
Columbia, SC
25 June 2021